CHIARA

IN THE

DARK

MAYA CHHABRA

An imprint of Enslow Publishing

WEST **44** BOOKS™

Please visit our website, www.west44books.com.
For a free color catalog of all our high-quality books,
call toll free 1-800-398-2504.

Cataloging-in-Publication Data

Names: Chhabra, Maya.
Title: Chiara in the dark / Maya Chhabra.
Description: New York : West 44, 2022. | Series: West 44 YA verse
Identifiers: ISBN 9781978595958 (pbk.) | ISBN 9781978595941
(library bound) | ISBN 9781978595965 (ebook)
Subjects: LCSH: Children's poetry, American. | Children's poetry,
English. | English poetry.
Classification: LCC PS586.3 C443 2022 | DDC 811'.60809282--dc23

First Edition

Published in 2022 by
Enslow Publishing LLC
29 East 21st Street
New York, NY 10011

Editor: Caitie McAneney
Designer: Katelyn E. Reynolds

Photo Credits: Cvr, pp. 1–192 (background) Ruslan Shevchenko/
Shutterstock.com; cvr, p. 1 (font) Atstock Productions/
Shutterstock.com.

Printed in the United States of America

CPSIA compliance information: Batch #CW22W44: For further information contact
Enslow Publishing LLC, New York, New York at 1-800-398-2504.

For Katherine

FREEDOM

I am
gliding
over the ice.

My best friend
clings
to the wall.

But I am
free.
No hands,

no worries,
just
me.

Going so
fast,
wind in my hair.
Nothing
can
stop me.

1

FEAR

Olivia is afraid.
She hasn't gone ice-skating before.
She's got a puffy, white coat
and a thick, sky-blue scarf.
I just wear a light jacket.

She steps carefully along the wall,
hanging on.

"How are you doing that?"

I'm skating backward very quickly.

"Try letting go of the wall.
I'll hold your hands."

We zoom down the ice.
I go backward, she goes forward.

PAIRED UP

We are not at all like
the skaters who go in pairs at the Olympics.

We are slower.
Easier.

No one is lifting anyone else
above their head.

But we have a rhythm
as Olivia picks her way forward
and I glide backward, holding her hands.

It's the rhythm you get
when you've been best friends so long
you trust each other with everything.
With your life.

FEAR AGAIN

This time it's me.

We are in the rhythm of it all
and I imagine the worst.

For no reason.

Not on purpose.

I think:
what if we fall?

BLOOD ON THE ICE

What if she falls on my blade?
Because I made a mistake?
Because I wasn't careful enough?

What if her scarf catches
and breaks her neck?

What if she falls
and hits her head
and the ambulance has to come?

The ambulance takes her to the hospital,
but she doesn't wake up.
And she's dead.

And it's all my fault.

SHAKING

Shaking my head
side to side to clear it.
To clear away the blood
and the fear.

To shake it out of me.

"Watch out!"
Olivia calls.
I almost hit someone.
In my fear of an accident,
I almost made one happen
for real.

"I think we should go back
to how we were before."

SHRUGGING

Olivia shrugs
and grabs the wall again.
The boards. That's what we call it
at the skating rink
where I have lessons.

Olivia must think
how weird I'm acting.
Maybe she's mad at me.

But she doesn't let on.
She shrugs and moves on.

MOVING ON

And I move on, too.

This is good. This break
from senior year
and thinking about college
and thinking about what comes next.

When I'm skating, I don't worry about that.

I don't even worry too much
about what's wrong with my head:

How everything seems too real.
Even things that never happened.
How I have to shake the pictures out.
Let them fall back to blankness.

HOME

I get off the subway.
Back to Brooklyn
from the rink in Manhattan.

I pass the gyro shop.
And the dance studio I went to as a kid,
before I focused on skating.
The stalled construction site
that's been promising condos
for three years now.
The little corner bodega.
I want to get a drink,
but I'm almost home
where water's free.

Then our building.
I take the elevator
to the seventh-floor apartment.

Mom works from home
doing people's taxes.
Dad gets home later
from the hospital where he works
as a chemist in the lab.
We make a long-distance call
to Dad's family in Italy.

Everything is calm and safe and normal.

ON THE FIFTH FLOOR

Two floors down live the Guptas.
They have a kid, Julie.
Mom is the only other Indian in the building.
(And me too, although
no one would guess it from my name.)

We're friends.

Mrs. Gupta hired me to babysit last summer.
Julie is about two.
The terrible twos, they say.
Her parents never get a break
except when I look after her.

Mrs. Gupta is so skinny
you'd think she has no time to eat.
Mr. Gupta always seems
like he's in a hurry.

But they're nice people,
and I don't mind babysitting.

SKATING CAMP

That's the prize
for babysitting.

If I earn some money this year,
Mom and Dad will pay the rest.

They're not really sure
why I want to go to a college
with a good ice-skating team.

Why I care so much about a sport.

But they pay for my lessons.
And if I help out Mrs. Gupta,
and keep my grades up,
they'll help with camp, too.

My grades aren't bad.
Well, they're not like Olivia's.
Olivia can tell you
exactly what she wants to study
(history)
and where
(Columbia).

But I do just well enough
that my parents won't nag me.

DINNER DATE

Today the Guptas have a dinner date.

So around six I head over.
Julie is throwing a tantrum.

WAH!

      AHHH!

NO-NO-NO!

Her toys lie all over the floor–
a doll and a whole box of blocks
tipped over.

She really doesn't want them to go.

But the clock is ticking
closer to dinnertime.

So they have to leave anyway.

FUN AND GAMES

As I put the blocks back in their box:

"Do you want me to read you a book?"

> "No."

"Do you want to watch a movie?"

> "No."

"Not even your favorite movie?"

> "No, I don't want–"

(Quick, before she starts crying again–)

"Want to help me cook dinner?"

> A little, tiny bit of a smile.

HELPING

She doesn't really help, of course.
But I give her a bowl and a spoon to play with.
She drums out a song with them.

She is very loud.

Maybe I was that loud as a little kid, too.

As she sings to herself, I think:

One day, far away from now–
I'd want to have a baby like that.

THE WORST THING

I am chopping onions when the worst thing happens.

I don't know how to explain it.

Or what it is.

It's like what happened with Olivia.

Only much worse.

Much, much worse.

THE KNIFE

I keep imagining

    (This is my imagination, right?)

the knife that I am chopping onions with

sliding right between Julie's tiny ribs.

BEING IN MY BODY

My face is hot.

I touch it with my hand,
feeling the warmth.

To do this,
I have to put the knife down.

I put it down carefully,
as if it might jump up
on its own.

I CANNOT

I cannot chop onions anymore.

I cannot make dinner. We will have to get takeout.

I cannot look at Julie. Or else I see the same thing again.

I cannot tell anyone what's wrong. There's no one to tell.

I cannot stay here. But there's nowhere to go.

I cannot be this person anymore.

EVIL

Because the kind of person I am
is a bad person.

Only a bad person
would think of hurting a kid.

I can never tell anyone.
No one would understand.
No one *should* understand.

Even though part of me is saying,
It's not my fault. It just came to me.

And after all, I didn't do anything.

ALL I KNOW

I don't want it to happen again.

I shake my head side to side.
Like I did with Olivia.
Trying to get what's left of the image
out of my head.

Maybe I'm just being dramatic.
I'm not a murderer.
I've never really hurt anyone.

I don't want to start.

But it follows me around,
this picture in my head.
As if it were whispering:

Do it.

A LONG TIME

That's how long I have to pretend.
That's how long I have to not scare Julie.

(Maybe she *should* be scared of me?)

That's how long it takes to get Julie to sleep.
She cries so loud it's like she knows–
Even though all she knows is that her parents
still aren't home, and she doesn't want to sleep.

That's how long it takes for the Guptas to get home.

SORRY

They don't know what I'm sorry for,
or why I have to get home so fast.

I tell them I can't babysit for them anymore.

Mrs. Gupta's head tilts and
Mr. Gupta pulls off his glasses to clean,
like he can't be seeing me right.

But before they can say anything,

I'm gone.

NOT ASLEEP

I shut my eyes and it comes back.

This is stupid.
I'm being a drama queen.
Nothing happened.

Then why won't it go away?
Why won't it let me sleep?

When I wake up, it will be gone.
It has to be.

I can't even say what *it* is.

RED EYES

Dark circles under them.

Jaw dropping to let out a yawn.

Today's Saturday. No school.

It's okay that I'm not okay.

I have a skating lesson later.

Time to relax.
Then, time to glide
away from all this.

RELAXING IS HARD

I pull up a yoga video from online.
Try to do the stretches and poses perfectly.

It's not relaxing.

I try to count my breaths, in and out.
I try to meditate like my grandparents always say to.
I try just falling back on my bed, half-asleep.

Nothing undoes the knot,
not even falling asleep.

"CHIARA? YOU'RE LATE!"

"Aren't you supposed to be on the subway by now?"
Mom asks.

She has a line between her eyebrows.

"Why are you asleep?
It's almost one o'clock.
Don't you have skating?
Didn't you want to go to
skating camp this summer?
You keep telling us
how much you love it.
How you want to go to a college
with a good team."

Her voice seems to come
from a long way away.

RUSH

Grabbing my skate bag,
running for the train,
taking the last seat.

I can finally relax.
I am on my way.

In half an hour,
I will hear nothing
but my coach's directions
and the roar in my ears.

SO SHARP YOU COULD CUT YOURSELF

I am lacing up my skates.

The blades are dull
and need to be sharper.
I will take them to the store
after my lesson,
which I am late for.

The blades are dull,
but they catch the light
like the knife last night.

No.

Not now.

WHAT MY BRAIN DOES

It gets stuck, like a car that won't start,
like a key that won't turn.

I can't think of anything else.

If I wander away from the thought
of what happened last night,
it comes back after a minute,
before I even know it's there.

And who gets stuck
on thoughts of blood
and hurting people
and people dying?

I DIDN'T DO ANYTHING

I keep telling myself that.

But how long
until I do?

I GO HOME

"I'm feeling too sick to do anything,"
I tell my coach.

I am sick. Only a sick person
would think these things
about Julie,
who is only a little kid
and helpless.

But if I'm sick, is it my fault?

BACK AND FORTH

I didn't do anything bad.

But what if you do?

I would never hurt anyone.

Then why can't you stop thinking about it?

Because it's disturbing.

And not normal.

You try acting normal with a horror movie in your head.

Do normal people have those?

On and on and on,
the sides of me arguing.

ON THE WAY HOME

I miss my stop.

I miss my life.

I miss my sanity.

I miss knowing for sure that I am good.

I watch the train pull away.

My sick mind wonders what it would be like
to be crushed by those wheels.

It didn't used to be like this.

I try to brush away the scary thoughts like I did
when I went skating with Olivia.
Brush them away, like the thoughts of her falling.

But these ones won't let go.

QUESTIONS

"Why are you home early?

Why didn't you go to your lesson?

What do you mean, you're sick?

Do you have a sore throat?

A fever?

What kind of illness?"

I shut the door.

I CAN'T TELL

If anyone knew, they would lock me up
for everyone's safety.

If Mrs. Gupta knew,
she'd be afraid of me,
disgusted.

If Olivia knew,
she wouldn't want to be alone with me.
(And it's not like I have a ton of friends.)

If my parents knew,
they would be destroyed.

But the truth is,
if I told anyone,
I would break into tiny pieces.

It's not them I'm afraid of.

It's my own words.

It's me.

I MAKE A PLAN

I will stay far away from Julie.

I will stay far away from knives.

And trains. Add trains to the list now.

(Which is impossible in New York.)

But still.

I will even stop skating for a while.

Yes, I need to be good to try out for college teams.

But a little break won't hurt.

Maybe if I stay away from everything,

everything that hurts,

it will stop hurting.

NOTHING

Mom says,
"Do you need to talk to someone?"

Dad says,
"You've been acting strange, Chiara.
Is something going on?"

My throat closes like I'm about to cry.

Nothing, Mom. Nothing, Dad.

Maybe if I say it out loud, it will be real.

SUNDAY IS A BLUR

So is Monday.

I go to school and smile so hard my face hurts.

I sit in front because that's where Olivia likes to sit.
I can't even answer half the questions on a quiz.
Usually school isn't this hard.
Usually I can get by with less effort
than I put into sports.

Olivia doesn't notice. She's too busy arguing with
our AP Euro teacher about Napoleon.
He's wrong about the Battle of Leipzig.
Finally, he agrees with Olivia,
not that I can really get excited about it.

Please. I'm not okay. How can you not see it?

But then again,

how can I blame her?

I'm hiding it from her.

Hiding so hard my head hurts.

SHOULD

If I really am sick, I should get help.

That's what they always say: get help.

I don't really believe anyone can help.

A WHOLE WEEK
SLIDES BY

I almost fail a calculus quiz.
And "almost fail" looks like failure
to my parents, who were both good enough
at school to come to the U.S. for college
from their home countries.

But it's a great excuse when I say
I want to take a break from skating
to concentrate on school.

My dad's eyebrows climb up, up, up—
like he doesn't believe me.
Like I'm a weird result
under his microscope
in the chem lab.
But he says nothing.
After all, wasn't my focus on school
what my parents wanted?

I understand now why people say nothing.
It's so much easier.

I GO OUT LIKE A NORMAL PERSON

Olivia and I go see some stupid movie.
All superheroes in bright stretchy costumes.
I drink a giant milkshake
and we talk about…nothing, really.

It's so easy.

I'm not good at making friends,
and neither is brainy Olivia,
but we click together.

I almost forget
my problems
by the time I'm walking
into the lobby of my building.

Then,
there's Mrs. Gupta chatting with Mom.

PLEASE DON'T SEE ME

Please don't talk about me.

Please don't think about me.

I'm not here.

I ALMOST MAKE IT

I am almost at the elevator
when Mom looks up and says,
"Chiara! How was the movie?"

Mrs. Gupta looks up too,
right at me,
and says,
"Julie misses you, but I know
you're too busy with school
to babysit."

And Mom tilts her head.

"What?"

I DON'T HEAR WHAT SHE SAYS

I run,
taking the stairs
up six flights.

I can't breathe,
but even more,
I can't stay.
I can't listen.

LOCKED DOOR

I get a few minutes' peace
before Mom starts knocking.

"Chiara, what's wrong with you?"
"Chiara, that was so rude!"
"Chiara, are you okay?"

EVERYTHING I'VE LOST

As she knocks, I think of everything that's gone now:

-my babysitting job
-my chance of saving money for skating camp
-skating itself
-my parents' trust
-my sanity

How much more do I have to give up
to keep people safe
from me?

UNFAIR

I didn't do anything wrong.

But if I really did nothing,
then why is this happening to me?

Was I bad all along—
violent, cruel—
and I just didn't know?

THE KNOCKING STOPS

And I hear low voices.
Mom and Dad's voices.
I can't hear what they're saying,
and I don't want to know.

IT COMES BACK

What if I killed my whole family and myself
and I never had to deal with this again?

I could.

I can see it.

The scary thing is:
it takes a long, long second
for me to remember
how evil that would be.

GO AWAY

It doesn't go away,
or it does, but only halfway.

The thought is like a scratch
on sunglasses.

I can see everything else.
But I can still see the scratch, too.

ROUND AND ROUND

I would never, ever do that.

> But you thought about it.

But I know it's wrong!

> But it took you a bit to remember that.

This isn't real. I'm making this up. This can't be my life.

> But it is.

DEEP BREATHS

don't help.

Help. I need help. I can't do this on my own.

I need to tell someone before I do something terrible.
Before I hurt someone I love.

I am afraid of talking about it.
But there are things I am more afraid of.

I STUMBLE OUT OF MY ROOM

Into the kitchen. Mom and Dad
stop talking when they see me.

They look like they're scared.
Like they're going to cry even.

I make myself say it.

"I think I need to see a doctor.
I think I'm going crazy."

AND THEN I DO NOTHING

My parents call their friend
whose son had a breakdown last year
and ask who he's seeing.

Then they make an appointment for me.

I do nothing. I just sit there.

I don't know how I'm going to do this.

"YOU SHOULD BE PROUD OF YOURSELF."

That's what they say.

But I'm not.

I'm just scared.

"DO YOU WANT TO HANG OUT?"

Olivia asks
at my locker.
She ties her thick, sky-blue scarf
around her neck.
She's already wearing it in fall,
always feeling chilly.
Plus, it's the school color
for Columbia University.
She wears it like a wish.

"Sorry, I have skating," I lie.

Olivia frowns.

"I thought that was tomorrow."

"I changed the day," I lie. "Getting ready for a big test."

Today is my first therapy session.

I feel like Olivia can tell I'm lying.

I'm afraid she can't.

THE DOORWAY

I tell my parents I can go alone.
I can. I can.
They aren't happy about it.
They wanted to come with me.
They're worried.

The door to the office has a code lock.
I have the code on my phone.
It takes two minutes for me to move my hand to the
keypad.
Another minute to tap the numbers in.

The door doesn't open.

Okay, I think. I tried.
I can leave.

But I check the email again.
It says to tap the pound sign after the code.

No more excuses.

THE POINT

"So why are you here?"

Emma Li, the therapist, gets to the point
much faster than I thought.

After I have filled out the last of a million forms,
signed my name over and over.
Chiara Benedetti, Chiara Benedetti.
After we have done the "tell me about yourself" thing.

She just asks me straight out.

Why are you here?

I THINK ABOUT LEAVING

But I've come this far.

And if I go back, this will keep eating my life
till nothing's left for me but crumbs.

I want to tell her.

I can't tell her.

I have to tell her.

Even if my throat is closing up,
and I'm not sure I can talk.

WRITING IT DOWN

"I can't say it," I tell her.
"Can I write it?"

Emma or Ms. Li,
I'm not sure what to call her,
passes me a notepad.

I think I will just write in big letters:

I HAVE BAD THOUGHTS ABOUT HURTING PEOPLE.

But instead I write pages,
the whole story,
how it started and won't stop.

I write till my hand cramps.
I don't read over what I wrote.
I shut my eyes and pass it back.

SHE READS IT

My skin crawls as I watch her.
Then she looks up.
Tells me, "Thank you for telling me,"
and hands me a list of questions.

*Do you experience unwanted thoughts that you find
horrifying or shameful?*

Yes.

Do you have a strong fear of germs?

No.

Do you check things over and over?

No.

Do you fear your bad thoughts will come true?

I tick that one off so hard the pencil goes through the
paper.

O C D

"What was that survey for?"
I ask.

She is still looking at it.

"Ms. Li…"

"You can call me Emma.
And that was a survey
of symptoms for
Obsessive-Compulsive Disorder."

I laugh.
"You mean the cleaning thing?
I'm so messy."

"Not everyone with OCD cleans things.
And those who do clean
do it because they have thoughts.
Thoughts they think are bad.
Thoughts they will do anything to stop."

I stop laughing.

BUT I DON'T DO ANYTHING

I don't sort things or wash my hands.

I don't do anything to stop the thoughts.

I would, but I don't know how to stop them.

Emma says, "You stopped babysitting,
you stopped going skating,
you avoid anything that makes it happen.

And there's another thing you wrote about.
How you think about it over and over
in circles in your head,
like if you thought enough, it would go away.

That's doing something."

THE MOST
IMPORTANT THING

"The thing you have to know, Chiara,
is that you'll never do any of these horrible things
in real life.

These thoughts will never leave your brain.

They're called intrusive thoughts.
They come when you don't want them,
because you don't want them.

But they're just thoughts.

Julie is safe. Your family is safe.
You're safe."

HOW DO YOU KNOW?

"What if you're wrong, though?
What if I'm just a bad person
who wants to hurt people,
and sooner or later, it will happen?

Sooner or later, I'll do something awful,
something there's no going back from."

I am almost in tears.

Emma says,
"Chiara, if you really wanted to do it,
you wouldn't be so upset."

BREATHING

"Oh, thank God."

That's all I say,
but the fear in the back of my mind
relaxes.

I have told someone,
and it is more real now.
But it's also less scary.

I'm not going to hurt anyone.

And Emma knows what this is,
and maybe she knows
how to make it go away.

"SO HOW DO I GET RID OF IT?"

That's the next question.
How do I make it stop?

Because I don't want to live with
a horror movie playing in my head,
even if no one gets hurt.

Emma says, "The more things you do to stop it,
the more things you avoid,
the stronger it gets.

But there is a therapy that works.
For many people, anyway.

I'm not trained.
But I can send you to someone who is."

ALL FIRED UP

I'm ready,
ready to do anything
to get better.

After all,
I faced all my fears to get here,
to get answers.

How hard can it be
to go to a different therapist,
to talk it out some more?

I am ready. So ready.

Then Emma tells me more.

TRIGGERS

When you go to ERP
(that's the name of the therapy),
you have to face your triggers.

Over and over again,
till they don't bother you so much.

"What are triggers?" I ask.
I feel like I've heard of them,
but I don't know what they are.

Emma explains,
"Whatever makes you have those thoughts,
whatever reminds you of them.
The point is to make the thoughts
lose their power,
let them pass
without doing anything to stop them."

SO BASICALLY

"So you want me
to have those thoughts on purpose?
Over and over again?"

I can't do that.
Not even if it will make me better.

"Maybe I can do that later," I say.

Emma says, "Whenever you're ready."

ONLY MAKES IT STRONGER

"Avoiding my triggers
will make it worse, right?
So maybe I should go back to skating."

I'm a little scared
because last time I tried, it was bad.

"Do things at your own pace," Emma says.
"I'll give you a book to read
about OCD and how it works.
It's not homework,
but you might find it helpful."

The clock ticks to the end of our meeting.

ALMOST BOUNCING

down the hall to the elevator,
holding the book Emma gave me.

I have a name
for what's happening to me.

I will learn
all about how it works.

I won't let it
ruin my life.

I start the book
on the subway home.

And it says there in black and white,
in the chapter on violent thoughts
(which is only one kind of scary thought
you can have),
that they never come true.

I'll never hurt anyone.

I READ

about people who clean
because they think their mother will die
if they don't do everything perfectly.

And people who check the gas stove
all the time
because they keep having thoughts
of the house exploding.

And people who worry all the time
about right and wrong
and what God will think,
even when it doesn't make sense.

And people who are scared
they will hurt their own children,
even though they would rather die.

who think they are bad,
who think they will
say racist things to their friends,
so they avoid them.

There are people
who think they might
crash their car on purpose
and kill themselves
or someone else.

And there are people
who think they will do something
so awful they can't speak it,
like rape or murder.

I GUESS I AM ONE
OF THEM

I'm one of these people
with these thoughts.

I looked at the kid I was babysitting
and saw her dead.
I looked at my parents,
and I wondered what would happen
if I couldn't stop myself.

But I'm not going to kill Julie
or my family
or anyone.

It says so right here in this book.

HUGS

My parents give me a big hug
when I get home,

and I give them the bill
Emma gave me.

On it is a little billing code
that says OCD.

"But you're so messy!
How can you have OCD?"

And I wave the book
and say,

"It's more complicated than that."

MY PARENTS

want to know everything.
Want to know how they can help.

"Shouldn't we talk to your therapist
so we know what's going on?"

I may have been able to
tell Emma what was going on,
in writing at least,
but no way will I tell my parents.

"You can read the book,"
I say, knowing there's no way they can tell
from a book
what my thoughts are.

Other people might not understand.
They might think I really could hurt someone.
They might think what I thought–
that I'm a bad person.

Even if they didn't,
they'd be really freaked out.

Imagine if Mrs. Gupta knew
why I stopped babysitting.

I can't imagine telling
even Olivia
or my parents.

But that's okay.
I'm okay.
I know what I'm doing.

FIRST THINGS FIRST

The first thing I can fix
is skating.

That's the easiest thing,
and I miss it.

It's not like babysitting,
which I'm still scared of.

So I might not earn enough
to go to the skating summer camp
I wanted. Too bad.

I'm not going back to the Guptas.

But I am going back
to the ice.

BY MYSELF

I don't go for a lesson.
Too much pressure.

I go by myself
at a time when the rink
is full of people.

People snacking outside,
people falling inside,
people tying their skates
beside me.

No one sees me
or knows
or cares.

I'm just one more person
taking too long on the bench
before going in.

MY SKATES ARE SHARP

I had them fixed nicely
at the shop
so the blades
have edges.

I couldn't actually cut myself
on the edges
without trying.

They wouldn't actually make
a good knife,
now that I think about it.

And I feel the whole world slipping
as the thoughts start again.

MAYBE I CAN'T

Maybe I should just go home now.

Maybe I tried too soon.

I don't have to do it today.

Just because I can't right now
doesn't mean I never will.

But I am so, so tired
of giving up bits of my life
so these thoughts will stay away.

I GET ON

I go twice around the rink,
nothing fancy
because there are too many people.

It's not as long as a lesson, either.

But I get that rush all the same,
wind through my tied-back hair,
even though I can't go very fast
with so many people around.

I slip and almost fall, but I catch myself.

It hasn't been that long.
I can catch up.
I can do this.

WINNING

When I get outside,
I am almost skipping.
My bag hits my legs,
but I don't mind.

I don't mind anything right now.

This is the first step,
the first win,
on the way back to normal.

I SEE EMMA ONCE A WEEK

I tell her about going skating again,
and how I froze up,
but I didn't stay frozen up.

After that, I go back to my skating lessons.
I learn new moves.
Prepare for the next test.

It almost feels like before,
except sometimes
when all I can think about
is how it's not.

I still get those flashes
of violent pictures in my mind.

Sometimes it ruins my whole day.

I'M STILL AFRAID

Not of doing anything bad,
but of anyone finding out.

And I'm afraid of the feelings I get
when the thoughts come.

Sometimes I shake them off.

But other times,
they take over everything
until the only thing I can do
is lie in bed, hoping they stop.

TRAPPED

"Why are you afraid
of these feelings?"
Emma asks.

"They hurt," I say.
"They hurt my head.

Even though I know they're not real,
they won't go away.
And it's like being trapped
in a room with someone you hate
as they talk on and on
about terrible things."

ANOTHER OFFER

"I can refer you
for ERP if you want."

Emma doesn't push me
or judge me,
but I can tell she thinks
it would be a good idea.

"I don't think I'm ready,"
I say.

And I don't.
I'm not ready to go through these thoughts
over and over
but on purpose this time.

Why would I do that
if I didn't have to?

THERE ARE STILL
THINGS I CAN'T DO

I try not to help cook anymore
because there are knives everywhere
and no one seems to see the danger.

I know now I'm not the danger.
But it still feels that way
when I look at the sharp steak knives
and see them
going through Mom's flesh.

NOT PERFECT

So things aren't perfect.
They aren't back to normal.

But they're better than they were before.

My parents cut me some slack
when I have to be by myself
trying to flee whatever's causing this.

They don't understand,
not completely,
because I haven't told them,
and they worry.

But things are mostly okay.

OLIVIA DOESN'T KNOW

It's the biggest thing about me
that she doesn't know.

I feel bad,
lying to my friend
about why we can't hang out on Tuesdays.
Pretending everything's normal
and my life hasn't changed.

But it's nice
to have someone who doesn't know.

It's like a bit of before
that's still here,
that's still good.

SOMETIMES I WATCH

the skating team
from my dream college
online.

I see their shiny dresses flow
as they move with perfect timing,
turning at the same second,
weaving in and out.

I've never been on a team,
only skated alone.
Which is why I wanted to go to that summer camp.
I wanted to catch up,
to see if I could do it.

No chance of that now.

OR IS THERE?

I could talk to my parents.
But how can I explain
why I let Mrs. Gupta down?

Still: I'm back on the ice,
and as I watch the team move as one,
I think,
maybe next year I'll be one of them.

I'M COMING BACK
FROM SCHOOL

My brown skin is flushed pink
with the cold. I think my calculus test
went well, or at least
not badly.

Winter's on its way,
and it's not much warmer outside
than it would be at the ice rink.

Outside the building,
I see an ambulance.
What-ifs race through my mind.

I feel a little better when I see
that it's Mrs. Gupta standing next to it,
and then I feel bad about that,
because it may not be my family
but it's *someone*.

What if Julie's sick or hurt?

AN EMERGENCY

"I'm so glad you're here."

Mrs. Gupta grabs me,
and I almost drop
my backpack, heavy
with math textbooks.

"My husband fell down the stairs,
and I think his leg is broken.
Can you watch Julie
while I go with the ambulance?
Mrs. Lopez next door is watching her now,
but she can't stay long.
If you help out,
I can go with my husband."

I freeze up.

"Thank you so much, Chiara,"
she says, as if I agreed,
and gets in the ambulance.

I stare after it.

SOMEONE HAS TO DO IT

And if no one stays with Julie,
Mr. Gupta will be in the hospital
alone, with no help.

I have to watch her.

I text my parents,
telling them what happened.

And then I get in the elevator.
I am strong.
I can do this.

IF I AVOID IT

my OCD will only get stronger.

That's what I think
as the elevator goes up
to the fifth floor.

I am doing the right thing.

But I see the doorway,
and I remember last time,
and I think:
Is that enough
to protect me?

MRS. LOPEZ HANDS OFF JULIE

who is a little worried,
looking down,
not bouncing.

"Daddy fell,"
she says.
"Where's Mommy?"

"Daddy's going to be okay,"
I say.
"Mommy went to the doctor with him.
I'm going to stay with you
until she comes back."

So far, my brain doesn't hurt.

WE PLAY

She takes out her dolls
and pretends to be a doctor
with her little plastic kit.

"This one's sick,"
she says.
"But I'll fix it."

I wish it was that easy
in real life.
I wish she could fix
Mr. Gupta's broken leg

or my broken brain.

THERE ARE
LEFTOVERS

so I just heat dinner up.
No cooking. No knives.

It's going great.
I even remember
how I used to like babysitting.

How I used to think:
when I'm older,
I'll have my own baby
to take care of.
Maybe two.

And they'll trust me
like Julie trusts me now.

MISTAKE

But she shouldn't trust me,
some part of my mind screams.
What if I hurt her?

And it all comes back
in a big rush.

Don't think about it,
I tell myself.
*Don't go round and round
in your head
about if this makes you
evil.*

You know it doesn't.
You know it's not real.

IT TURNS OUT

knowing it's not real
doesn't do anything.

Doesn't stop it,
doesn't make it better,
doesn't do anything at all.

I CAN'T STAND

how much it hurts.

I put my head in my hands,
rub my eyes,
trying to push the pictures away.

Nothing works.

I TRY NOT THINKING ABOUT THEM

Think about your job.
Think about skating camp.
Think about how glad Mrs. Gupta was
when she realized she could go with her husband.
Think about the good thing you're doing.

And I do. For a few minutes, I do.
And then I realize
I'm still thinking about
how easily I could hit Julie over the head
with the shoe stand.

BUT THIS ISN'T WHAT I WANT

I am screaming inside.

I don't want to hurt her.
I don't want to hurt anyone.
Why won't these thoughts leave me alone?

Julie finishes dinner
and asks if she can watch a movie.

I say yes,
even though I know she's not supposed to
watch TV right before bedtime.

THE MOVIE IS
A MISTAKE

For about half an hour Julie's quiet.
But then she starts to cry,
asking if Daddy's going to be okay
and why he didn't get up
when he fell.

I try giving her a hug
but she yells,
"I want Mommy!
Not you! Mommy!"

She pushes me away.

I KNOW IT'S STUPID

but what if she can tell
what's going on in my head?

What if she somehow senses
that I'm not safe?

It's stupid. She just wants her parents.
She'll stop crying sooner or later.

But what if?

IF MRS. GUPTA KNEW

she wouldn't care that I have OCD
or that I've never hurt anyone like that.

She'd see someone who shouldn't
be looking after her daughter.

Someone who shouldn't
live in the same building as her daughter.

Someone who shouldn't
be alive.

She trusted me.

I NEED TO GET OUT
OF HERE

Julie has stopped crying
and is watching the rest of the movie.

But it's a short movie,
almost over.

She'll figure it out.

She's two years old!
I tell myself.
*She's two and she's scared
because her dad's in the hospital.
She's not going to figure out anything
about what's in your head.
She'd have to be
a genius mind reader.*

I STILL NEED TO GET OUT OF HERE

I pull out my phone.
Look at my messages,
see if my parents are online.

I can't leave Julie alone,
but I can't stay with her either,
thinking of all the ways
I could kill her.

It's not even
that I'm afraid I'll do it.

I won't. I know I won't.

I just want this to stop.

BUT IF I ASK
MY PARENTS

to come, if I tell them
I can't look after Julie
because of my OCD,
then they'll know.

They'll figure out what it is.

They've read enough by now
to know OCD is all about
driving away the bad thoughts.

And if they know what causes mine,
what will they think of me?

I PUT AWAY
MY PHONE

I'm not going anywhere.

I'm going to fight my OCD.
Right here.
On its home ground.

JULIE DOESN'T WANT TO SLEEP

I read her favorite books to her,
and she smiles.
She knows these books by heart
and says the words along with me.

But then, when it's time
to turn the lights out,
she becomes
Julie of the Terrible Twos.

She wants more stories.
She wants a cup of milk.
She wants Mommy and Daddy.

She cries and cries.

I TRY TO BE GENTLE

I tell her that Mommy will be home
as soon as she can,
as soon as she's done
taking Daddy to the doctor,
who'll fix him up.

She doesn't believe me.

But after a long cry,
she puts her head on my shoulders,
and I give her a hug.

ALL THIS TIME MY BRAIN IS SCREAMING

how I could break her neck.

SHE'S ASLEEP

I hope.

I don't have anything to do now.

I hardly have any homework
now that we're about to hear back from colleges.

I have a book in my skating bag,
but it's boring.

I can relax.

But without anything to do,
I know what my brain will show me.

I TRY CALLING OLIVIA

"Hey,
what's up?"

But I don't know what to tell her
after lying to her this long.

I'm lucky. Because she's got news.
She just heard back from Columbia,
where she applied early.

She got in.

"It's such an amazing school!
And they're giving me a scholarship!
And I can stay right here in the city!"

I want to go far, far away
for college,

right now.

I WATCH A
SKATING VIDEO

I didn't apply early.
I won't hear back from colleges
for a while.

But there are a few I like better than others,
and I have the grades to get in.

Do I have the skills to skate with them, though?

Watching the teams,
I almost forget
everything going on tonight.

I'M JUST
FINISHING

the video
from Miami of Ohio,
the best team.

Watching them split
into three, four lines
and then cut through each other,
too fast to see,
all speed and grace.

I don't expect
Julie to come in
looking for water,
not wanting to sleep.

I PAUSE

help her get a sippy cup,
fill it with water for her.

My hands shake,
and the water spills,
but only a little bit.

WHEN I TAKE HER
BACK TO HER ROOM

she starts to delay.

"You have to sleep now,"
I say.
My mistake.

"Why?"
she asks,
again and again.
"Why?"

She gets on my nerves so much,
though I tell myself
she is two
and has had a hard day
and it's not her fault.

EVENTUALLY

she stops whining
and curls up around her pillow.

And my OCD goes:
the pillow that I could put over her–

No.

Not again.

So many different thoughts,
but they're all the same.

They're all
about hurting someone
I don't want to hurt.

Someone I want to protect.

EVEN THOUGH EMMA TOLD ME

and the book told me
and the internet told me
that I'm not a danger–

I don't really believe it.

Because I get out of there
as fast as I can
to protect her from me.

I CAN'T

I just can't.
I can't do this anymore.

I pull out my phone
and call my parents.

HELP ME

"I can't keep looking after Julie.
My OCD is too strong."

I'm afraid to tell them,
but I'm more afraid to stay.

"But what does your OCD
have to do with babysitting?"
Dad asks.

He wants to fix everything
like it's a problem in his lab.
At the hospital he runs tests,
and they tell him exactly what the matter is
so he can tell the doctors.

But I can't tell him.

I just say what I said before.

MRS. GUPTA CAN'T COME HOME YET

Mom says,

"Her husband's leg is still being fixed.
She wants to be there when he wakes up.

Please, hang on."

I can't hang on.
I'm tired of hanging on.

"Will you stay with her?
Please?"
I ask.
"I can't do it. It makes me too crazy.
It makes my head hurt."

"WHAT'S HAPPENING TO YOU, CHIARA?"

Dad asks.
"We can't help
if we don't know
what's going on."

I can't say it.
It gets stuck in my throat.

Okay, Chiara,
I tell myself.
*You have to find a way
to explain.*

Or you're stuck here.

REMEMBER THE BOOK

"Remember the book? It says
how with OCD
I have bad thoughts
and I'm always trying
to make them go away?"

"Yes,"
they say.

"This job makes my bad thoughts happen.
It's a, you know, a trigger."

Mom says,
"Oh, Chiara,"
and I think she knows
what I mean.

And Dad says,
"We'll come get you,
and we'll watch the kid
until Mrs. Gupta can come back."

I WAS SO SCARED

to tell anyone.

What if
they didn't understand?

And some people wouldn't.
Most people wouldn't.

But these are my parents.
They love me.
They want to help.

Why did I think I had to hide?

WAITING FOR
THE KNOCK

At the same time,
I feel like I gave up.

Like I just didn't try hard enough.
Like I could be normal if I really wanted it.

I'm leaving because I'm too scared
to do the job I should be doing,
too scared to help.

THEY'RE HERE

Mom catches me in a big hug,
and then Dad does the same.

And I let go. I'm safe.

Mom stays with Julie,
and Dad takes me back up
to our apartment
like I'm the one
who can't be left alone.

"WHEN I CAME HERE FROM ITALY..."

Dad says,
"before you were born,
before I met your mom,
I started to get really scared.

I was alone in a new country.

Maybe that's what set it off.

I couldn't talk to people
without feeling like I had to leave
right away
or I'd die of the feeling, the fear.

But it went away, in the end.
So I never thought it was important
to tell you about it.

But maybe something runs in the family,
some kind of anxiety.

I'm sorry."

"IT'S NOT YOUR FAULT."

I say.

"It would have happened to me
no matter what,
I think.

Even if it's a family thing,
that doesn't mean
that if you'd told me
anything would have changed."

A LIGHT

"Chiara, you are a light.
Your name means clear, bright, shining,"
Dad says.

"I feel like I live in the dark now,"
I say.

"You don't have to.
Maybe we didn't realize
how serious this was.
But we're going to help you."

Dad means it.

But I think
I'm the only one who can help me.

I know what I need to do.

I HAVE A FEW DAYS

till therapy.

A few days to choose.
But I've already chosen.

Emma told me
there's a therapy that can help,

and I didn't want to do it

because it sounded scary.

But what could be scarier
than being stuck in the dark
all the time
with no way out?

WHAT COULD BE SCARIER

than never getting over this?

Never being able to have kids
because I'd be too scared
of hurting them?

Never being free
of these thoughts
that maybe won't hurt
anyone else,
but they're hurting me?

What could be scarier
than what's already going on?

AND EVEN IF

I have to let myself
feel these thoughts
over and over
in therapy
to get rid of them,
so what?

I am scared.
But I can't let being scared
control my life forever.

I GO TO SLEEP

It takes a long time
to fall asleep.
I'm afraid I'll have bad dreams.

I am having bad dreams
while I am still awake,
with my eyes open.

So I might as well
just fall asleep.

And when I wake up,
Mrs. Gupta will be back,
and she'll talk to my mom.

I hope Mom can explain
without telling her everything.

I trust my family, though.
They came to help me.

MRS. GUPTA IS
NOT HAPPY

Or so Mom says
when she comes back.

"She doesn't want you
to babysit anymore
because she thinks
she can't count on you.

I tried to tell her it wasn't your fault,
but I didn't want to tell her
anything you weren't okay with sharing."

So I'm a flake
in Mom's friend's eyes.

And there will be no skating camp.
(But was there ever going to be a skating camp?)

IT'S TOO BAD

I say,
"I guess I need to find another job."

Mom says,
"Don't be silly.
Getting better is your job right now.
I know you wanted
to go do sports this summer–"

And I think she's going
to tell me how that doesn't matter.

But she says,
"Your dad and I
will help you with that camp
if you really want it.

You don't need a job.
You have enough going on."

SO I CAN GO

I can spend the summer
skating my heart out.

Why do I feel empty
instead of happy?

They've been so good,
but they don't know
how hard getting better will be.

How even if I try my hardest,
I might not ever get better.

I read that ERP therapy doesn't always work,
not all the way.
It just works better than anything else.

What if I try and try
and still end up stuck in the dark?

I SKIP SCHOOL
THAT DAY

After all,
I really am sick.

And even my parents,
who think I don't care enough
about school,
let me.

Olivia calls later.

"Hey, where were you?
Are you okay?"

I guess this is practice
for telling other people,
at least a little bit.

I say I've been going to therapy
for OCD,
and I had a bad brain day.

Olivia says,
"I don't exactly know what that means.
But you were here for me when my dad left.
And I'm here for you."

THE NEXT DAY
IS THERAPY

I tell Emma
I want her to send me
to the person
she talked about at the beginning.

I want to do ERP.

And she smiles
while printing out
the email and phone number.

She's proud of me, I think.

I TAKE THE FIRST APPOINTMENT I CAN GET

Everything—
my parents' worries,
Olivia's concern,
Mrs. Gupta's awkward stare
in the elevator—
everything is a blur.

I can think of only one thing.
Starting this new therapy
next week.

Of course,
I feel dread
at the thought
of having to explain
in detail.

But this will be a therapist
who's used to hearing
these things.

Who won't look at me funny
or tell anyone
or judge.

I hope.

I really hope.

HARD TO FOCUS

on my moves at skating.

I almost crash
into another girl,
who turns
at the last minute.

My coach isn't happy.

"Are you daydreaming, Chiara?"

But it's more like
day-nightmares.

If this doesn't work, will anything?

AT LAST

I'm here,
in the therapist's office,
with my mom waiting for me
in the waiting room.

Ms. Thomas
isn't like Emma.

She doesn't tell me
her first name.

She's more stiff,
and I'm a little scared of her
with her short, white hair
and her few words.

But I guess
she knows what she's doing.

TELL ME

There's less small talk
at the start.

Ms. Thomas jumps right in.

"So, Chee-ara."

And I tell her
that's not how you say my name,
it's more like "Kya-ra."

So that's not a great way
to begin.

But she fixes it
right away
and asks me,
"So, Chiara. Can you tell me
about your OCD?"

I'M GETTING BETTER AT THIS

I still want to ask for
paper and pen
like the first time I saw Emma.

But I'm not going to be afraid anymore.

I want my life back.

So in a small voice
I start to say,

"It began when I was babysitting…"

MS. THOMAS LISTENS

She doesn't say anything
until I'm done.

"Can you think of any other times
you've had feelings or thoughts like this
besides around Julie and your family?"

I think.

I remember, before any of this,
going skating with Olivia
and being afraid she'd fall and die.

"I think so."

"What do they all have
in common?"

I'M SCARED OF
HURTING PEOPLE

That's what I come up with
after thinking about it a little.

"Right," says Ms. Thomas,
"you have Harm OCD,
where your thoughts are about
the harm you could do to people.

You can't hurt people
in therapy,
of course."

"Of course," I laugh.

"But you have to face your fears."

I am not laughing anymore.

THERE ARE THINGS I CAN DO

Ms. Thomas tells me.

"Like recording yourself talking
about your worst thoughts

or picturing them
on purpose."

I'm shaking.

"We can work up to it.
Let's make a ladder
of things that are easy
all the way up
to the hardest.

We're not going to do them all today.
It will take weeks, months.

But I think you're up
to the challenge."

WHEN I LEAVE

with the ladder I drew
in my backpack,

I'm still upset.

But Mom is right here,
and we're going home.

And I don't have to do anything
until next week at least.

One more week
to rest
and recover
and get ready
for the battle.

THE FIRST WEEK

I just have to write things down.
Write
I am a killer
over and over again
until the words don't
mean anything anymore.

Afterward,
I crumple up the paper
and throw it out.

I want to tear it into tiny bits
so no one will ever see.
But who would go through the garbage,
anyway?

I force myself not to dig it out
and shred it.

I am making progress.

BUT I'M ALSO

stressed and worried.

I have to learn to deal with that
without doing anything about it.

Without trying to avoid
the things that make me stressed.

A normal person could,
and I'm jealous.

But the way my brain works,
avoiding things
only makes them worse.

When I ran away from Julie,
I was making it worse.

OLIVIA KNOWS

Not the details, but some things.
She always calls me
after I get out of therapy.

I'm lucky.

I've got a good friend,
a good family.

They would all do anything for me.

But they can't do this for me.

I have to.

AT SKATING

I'm finally back on track,
getting ready for my Senior Moves Test,
the hardest footwork test.

I can't wait to get the jacket
with my name on it in gold,
and the gold medal,
if I pass.

I can't wait to have made it to the top
of the skating test ladder,
even if it's not as hard
as the ERP ladder.

I DO ERP EVERY DAY

I'm better about it
than I am about homework.

And I do see
myself getting better,
like when I practice a spin at the rink
and slowly it gets easier.

But that's only
at this stupid game
of writing things down.

I don't think
I could babysit again.

Not yet.

THE NEXT LEVEL

I have to use a knife every day.

It's true,
I don't like to cook anymore
and avoid it if I can.

It's easier
if there's no one in the kitchen with me.

So the first week,
I do it alone,
and Mom and Dad are happy
that they don't have to cook.

And I'm happy
that there's no one else there.

Even though I know
they won't get hurt,
I'm afraid I will,
inside.

BECAUSE MY BRAIN IS WEIRD

With no one else around,
I start to have thoughts
of hurting myself.

The first time this happens
while I'm cooking,
I put everything down,
turn off the gas,
call Ms. Thomas right away.

Because I don't like chopping onions
and thinking of the blade
going straight to my wrist.

MS. THOMAS CHECKS

"Do you want to kill yourself
or hurt yourself,
or is it a picture in your mind,
a thought you can't get rid of?"

"I don't want to die,
I just want to finish cooking dinner,
but I'm too freaked out."

"You can stop if you need to.
Maybe this was too soon.
But I don't think you will hurt yourself.
I think it's your OCD twisting,
trying to find a new form."

"So if I avoid it,
it will get worse,
like all the rest of my OCD?"

"We might be pushing you too fast,
which doesn't actually help.
It's best to go slow with ERP.
But you're right.
Avoiding it won't help.
Avoiding is a compulsion."

"Thanks. Okay, I get it. Bye."

I GO BACK TO CHOPPING ONIONS

I'm winning.

I hate this, but I'm winning.

I'm not going to give up now.

Afterward I cry so much
that I can barely eat
the dinner I cooked.

THE NEXT WEEK

is using a knife with someone else around.

Which means I have to ask my parents
to cook with me.

I say it's for therapy.
Which is true.

When I asked Ms. Thomas if I had to tell them
the truth,
she said maybe I should do that at the end of the ladder
if I wanted to
but I didn't have to.

They sort of know,
and they love me,
and that's enough.

THE FIRST TIME I TRY

I can barely chop the carrots,
because I keep thinking.

In the corner of my mind,
like the corner of my eye,
I see blood.

I can't really look at the knife,
which isn't safe.

So I put it down for a second,
just a second.

But looking up, looking around,
seeing my mom is worse.

I go back to
the carrots and the knife,
forcing myself to look,
to be careful.

MEANWHILE, COLLEGE

I'm supposed to be
getting ready for college.

Olivia lets me read her essay
that got her into an Ivy.
She talks about her parents' divorce
and her love for history
and somehow weaves these two together.

All these essays ask:
What have you overcome?

I need to have a great story.
But my parents are together
and we have enough money
and I don't really have a passion
for any school subject.

I'm just overcoming my messed-up brain.

But I can't write about that.
They don't actually want to know,
do they?

Anyway,
I haven't overcome anything—
yet.

IT DOES GET EASIER

There are times
when I'm in the kitchen
and my mind
throws up images of murder.

And I think, *Okay, whatever,
you're not real,*

and move on.

There are also times
when nothing works,
and I have to keep going
with all the strength I have.

One day is so bad
that I end up skipping dinner,
crying in my bedroom.

After all that time cooking it, too.

My parents knock on the door,
but I keep it shut.

I just cry
until I fall asleep.

I'M ASHAMED

to tell my therapist about that,
but she says,
"You did it anyway.
See? You are up
to the challenge."

I don't feel up to anything,
but we decide
to repeat the last week
until it gets easier.

I get why,
even though I'm not happy.

BUT SECRETLY

it's okay that we're
repeating last week's ERP.

That just keeps me
a step longer away
from the last test.

Because the last
ladder step
is seeing Julie.

Easy enough.

Just go with Mom
when she goes to check
how they're doing
with Mr. Gupta's broken leg
and everything.

But so hard.

THE NEXT WEEK HELPS

I get to the point
where I can be holding a knife
and someone I love is nearby
and I don't freak out,
even inside.

Not too much, anyway.

It's not perfect,
but it's better.

And I'm not thinking about it every moment.
At school I mostly think about school.

I'm starting to believe,
that as much as I hate doing it,
this therapy will work.

I DO FREAK OUT

when we record
me saying all the ways
my mind thinks of killing people.

"What if someone finds this?
And thinks it's real?"

"You can erase it after a week,"
Ms. Thomas promises.

I'm still not sure about this.

I have to sit in my room
with earbuds
so no one else hears
while I listen.

I HATE LISTENING

but it's a different hate
each time.

At first it's because
my face flushes,
my fists clench,
my body goes into fight-or-flight.

Later it's because
it's boring.

I already know
every awful thing
in my head.

I don't need to hear it.

THAT MEANS IT'S WORKING

I'm confused.

Ms. Thomas says again,
"That means it's working.
That you get bored
instead of scared
listening to it."

"Is that what
it will be like afterward?"
I ask.
"I'll still have these thoughts,
but they'll be boring?"

I don't want them at all.
I want them gone.
I thought ERP might make them go away
forever.

SOMETIMES YES, SOMETIMES NO

Like the flower petal game
little kids play.
Loves me, loves me not.
It's chance.

Some people have no more
frightening thoughts,
and some people have them still.

"But,"
Ms. Thomas says,
"if this works,
they won't bother you anymore.
They'll be there,
but you'll know
how to deal with them."

Is that good enough?
After all this trying?
I don't know.

WE'RE AT THE END
OF THE LADDER

It's the dead of winter,
and I've somehow kept up
with college apps
and midterms
and therapy.

Kept up well enough to get here.

There's only one thing left.
Only one more challenge.
Only one more fear.

NEXT TIME MOM

goes to see the Guptas,
I ask to go with her.

She starts to ask something
but doesn't.

She's a little surprised
but happy.

I'M NOT HAPPY

I don't want to see them.

I'm sure
they don't like me anymore.

Not after I flaked out on them
when Mr. Gupta was in the hospital
and they needed help.

That's not the only reason
I don't want to go.

But it's one of them.

BUT I HAVE TO DO IT

And more than once.

I have to do it until
I'm not scared anymore.

Until I'm just bored
by the horrors
in my mind.

WE GET READY TO GO

Mom holds my hand tight
like I'm a little kid,
then drops it
as we get out
of the elevator.

She knows
this is hard for me.

And that makes it easier.

MRS. GUPTA IS SURPRISED TO SEE ME

Her face doesn't fall,
but she stops what she was saying
and stares.

I wonder
if she wonders
why I couldn't stay.

I hope she doesn't think
badly of me,
but maybe that's a lost cause.

WELCOME

She invites us in.

Julie is playing
on the floor
in a sea of LEGOs.

"Say hi, Julie,"
her mom tells her,
waving at us.

Julie waves for a second,
then goes back to her LEGOs.

So far, nothing.

MR. GUPTA IS
GETTING BETTER

Mrs. Gupta tells us,

"It was really scary at first.
He broke it in two places,
but now he's doing a lot better."

He has to do exercises every day
to help him get better.

I get that. It's not easy,
but it's better
than always being hurt.

WE HAVE TEA

Indian-style,
with warm milk and spices.

I'm starting to relax.

JULIE WANTS TO SAY HI

She walks up with her LEGO car,
right up to me,
and says,
in her small, hard-to-hear voice,
"Do you want to play?"

She holds the toy out to me.

AS SHE HOLDS IT OUT TO ME

in her tiny hand,
pictures slide through my mind.

Her arm is so small I could break it.

And I think,
it was all for nothing,
all this effort.

Because I'm right back where I started.

BUT I SAY

"Sure,"
and take the toy car
she made out of LEGOs.

I make it go vroom-vroom,
fast around her head.

She laughs and spins around,
trying to follow it.

And I realize
those thoughts have gone away.

OKAY

"You don't have to play with her
if you don't want to,"
Mrs. Gupta says.

"Oh, it's okay,"
I say, smiling.

"I know you didn't want
to keep babysitting her,"
Mrs. Gupta goes on, coldly.

"I'm sorry about that,"
I say,
and I mean it.

COME ON

Julie says,
pulling my arm.

"I want to show you
a giant tower
that I made."

She shows it to me,
and then she knocks it down,
shrieking with joy.

And I laugh
and help her pull the pieces apart.

EVERY SO OFTEN

the thoughts start to come back,
but then they fade.

I know what they are.

After listening to them all last week,
they seem…boring.

They don't bother me so much anymore.

WHEN WE LEAVE

Mom asks how it went,
if I'm okay.

She remembers
what I said that night.

"I'm okay, Mom,"
I say.
"I think therapy is working."

AT HOME

I let out a big breath.

I go watch a video
of the University of Michigan team
skating their way to gold
at Nationals.

I applied there last week.

Next year,
I'll be on my own,
somewhere far away.

I think I can handle it.

I CAN DO IT BECAUSE

after this, everything seems easy.

I don't know if I'm cured.
After all, the thoughts still come.
I still have to live with them.

Also, it was only one visit.
Maybe on the next one, I'll freak out.

I don't know if cured is even the point, though.
The point is, I feel better.

I don't have to live in fear,
avoiding people and places.

I don't have to worry
that I'm a monster.

And if it comes back,
I know what to do about it.

I'M FREE, AGAIN

Life isn't
           a smooth glide
                      without falling.

Sometimes
           it's more like
                      learning a new move

or a new jump
           and you fall
                      more than you land.

But every day
           you get stronger
                      as the past stops

holding you back.
           Sometimes free
                      is something

you have to fight for.

WANT TO KEEP READING?

If you liked this book, check out another book
from West 44 Books:

SURVIVE AND KEEP SURVIVING
BY MEL MALLORY

ISBN: 9781978595927

DAMAGE

Years ago, my paranoia
and delusions grew

like an invasive plant
in my mom's garden,

with vines that trailed
throughout our house

and coursed through
the entire town.

CHECK OUT MORE BOOKS AT:

www.west44books.com

An imprint of Enslow Publishing

WEST **44** BOOKS™

ABOUT THE AUTHOR

Maya Chhabra is a current student in the Vermont College of Fine Arts MFA program and a graduate of Georgetown University. Her first novel, *Stranger on the Home Front*, was released in 2021. Her short stories and poetry have appeared in anthologies and magazines, including *Daily Science Fiction*, *Strange Horizons*, and *PodCastle*. She lives in Brooklyn with her wife.